PUMPKIN GUTS
VERSUS THE
VAMPIRES

Adapted by Natalie Shaw

Simon Spotlight
New York London Toronto Sydney New Delhi

PUMPKIN GUTS
VERSUS THE
VAMPIRES

SIMON SPOTLIGHT

An imprint of Simon & Schuster Children's Publishing Division

1230 Avenue of the Americas, New York, New York 10020

This Simon Spotlight edition July 2019

TM & © 2019 Sony Pictures Animation Inc. All Rights Reserved.

All rights reserved, including the right of reproduction in whole or in part in any form.

SIMON SPOTLIGHT and colophon are registered trademarks of Simon & Schuster, Inc.

For information about special discounts for bulk purchases, please contact Simon & Schuster Special Sales at 1-866-506-1949 or business@simonandschuster.com.

Designed by Bob Steimle

Manufactured in the United States of America 0619 LAK

10 9 8 7 6 5 4 3 2 1

ISBN 978-1-5344-4045-6 (hc)

ISBN 978-1-5344-4044-9 (pbk)

ISBN 978-1-5344-4046-3 (eBook)

CHAPTER ONE

It all started one particularly spooky night at Hotel Transylvania, the hotel for monsters that Drac built to keep his family and other monsters safe from the human world. He ran it with the help of his sister, Lydia; his daughter, Mavis; and a crew of zombies, witches, and other monsters.

Monsters were boarding up windows, locking doors, and getting ready to hide out for the night. It was all part of a monster tradition.

Drac was away at the Vampire Council, but he sent a message to Mavis by carrier bat. She started to read it. Mavis knew her father so well, it was like he was there in her room. She could practically hear his voice. She even imagined a Drac-shaped shadow on the wall.

My dearest Mavis. Just checking in and stuff to, you know, remind you to stay

inside on this, the most dangerous night of the year! You wouldn't want to be cooked and eaten by a human! So you must never go out! Ever! EVER! Did I say ever?

Mavis looked up and sighed. "Three times," she said flatly.

Drac's letter continued:

Good. Now stay in your room, hunker down, and cling to the hope that daybreak will come. Love you!

Mavis muttered to herself, "I love you, Dad, but sometimes you take this lockdown a *bit* too far."

Mavis got up and walked out of her room. Correction: Mavis *tried* to leave, but a monster's giant purple tentacle wrapped around her to keep her

in her room! "Case in point," she added.

That was when Aunt Lydia arrived. "Young lady, you know you are to remain in your room. Absolutely no monsters are allowed out on this, the most dangerous night of the year."

Then the hotel's chef, Quasimodo, ran up, looking with disgust at a basket of fresh fruit he was carrying. "Madam Lydia," he said, "the fruit is still," he sniffed, "disgustingly fresh. We will have no zombie provisions for the coming Hallo—"

Lydia magically zipped his mouth shut—with an actual zipper—so he couldn't say another word. "We do *not* say the H-word," she reminded him through gritted teeth.

Mavis protested, "You can at least say 'Halloween' around me."

Monsters nearby screamed in terror upon hearing that word. Lydia froze them in place to keep them quiet. "Now look what you've done. You know very well what happens when you say that!" she yelled.

"Of course I know. I'm only reminded every year!" Mavis complained. "But what can possibly be so scary that we go on lockdown till sunrise?"

Lydia bent down to be closer to her niece's eye level and said calmly, "Some things are better left unknown," before floating away.

Mavis was determined that this was the year she would discover the truth.

After the giant tentacle released her, she headed back toward her room.

CHAPTER TWO

Mavis called her friends to her room. Soon Wendy, who was a green blob with pink hair; Hank, who was Frankenstein's son; and Pedro, who was a mummy, arrived.

"Thank you all for coming," Mavis told them.

"We're trapped in a boarded-up fortress. Where were we gonna go?" Hank asked.

Mavis ignored him. "Tonight we break free and learn the real story behind Halloween! Aren't you guys tired of being locked down without being told why? I've spent the last six Halloweens plotting out our escape. In exactly four minutes, Aunt Lydia will finish sealing off the hotel. Of course, there's still the matter of getting out unseen. . . ."

"Right. And you've tried like a million ways out before," Pedro pointed out.

"Yep. But we forgot about a million and one," Mavis said, nodding her head toward the bathroom.

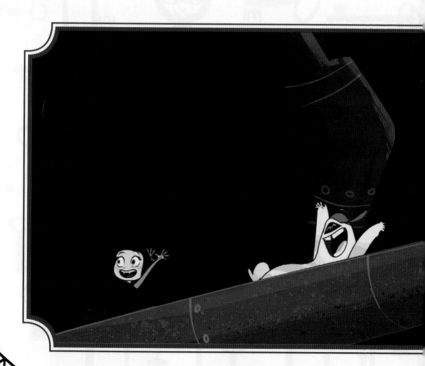

"Oh, no. No, no, no, no, no," Hank said. For a monster he was always a bit of a scaredy-cat. This time, Pedro and Wendy couldn't blame him for it.

They also couldn't convince Mavis to change her mind. Soon, the four friends were sliding down a drainpipe like it was a giant waterslide!

As the kids made their escape, a red skull-shaped phone rang in Lydia's office. It was the Vampire Council's emergency-only phone line. Lydia knew what that meant. She picked it up and said, "You want me to check on your little Mavy-Wavy?"

Sure enough, it was Drac calling. "No," Drac objected. "I want you to check on my little— Oh, I see what you did there. Now go check on her!"

Lydia carried the phone to Mavis's room,

expecting to find Mavis in her bed. Like all vampire beds, it was actually a casket. When Lydia looked inside, she saw a wolf pup sleeping. Mavis was gone!

"Mavissss . . . ," whispered a furious Aunt Lydia. Then she tried to cover up her discovery by telling Drac that Mavis was fast asleep and quickly hung up the phone.

Mavis and her friends were already in a human village near Hotel Transylvania. They were hiding in the bushes in front of someone's house.

Hank was confused. "Uh, Mavis, why are we creeping toward the human house?"

"Listen," Mavis told them. "Every year we're told

horror stories about what the humans are up to on Halloween. But what do we really know?" she asked.

They looked curiously at the house that was decorated with spooky spiders and skeletons. Wendy thought maybe the humans that lived there were having a party, but then she spotted two young monsters crossing the lawn. She was shocked!

"Holy rabies!" Wendy whispered to her friends. "Those monsters are walking right up to the door!"

Hank couldn't believe it, either. "She's gonna liquefy their organs and make a monster smoothie!"

They watched in horror as the monsters held out pumpkin-shaped baskets and said, "Trick or treat!" Their horror turned to surprise as a human smiled and dropped something into their baskets.

Wendy was confused. "I thought humans devoured monsters on Halloween?" So did Hank, Pedro, and Mavis.

They watched as one of the monsters lifted up his mask to get a better view of what was inside his basket. But the little monsters weren't monsters after all. They were *humans* dressed like monsters! The humans smiled and then walked to the next house.

Mavis didn't know why the humans were dressed as monsters, but she *did* know they got something good in those baskets. She wanted to try it too. She just needed some kind of bag. Mavis took a potted plant from the lawn and dumped out the plant. She brought the pot with her to the front door and held it out like a trick-or-treat bag. Then she knocked on the door!

The human opened the door and waited for Mavis to say the magic words.

Mavis tried to remember what the humans had said to get the treats, then mumbled, "Stick of meat?" under her breath.

Hank, Wendy, and Pedro watched from the bushes, expecting the worst.

"You," the human said to Mavis, "are the most darling little vampire. Such disgusting creatures." She dropped something into Mavis's bag and said, "Happy Halloween!"

Mavis ran to her friends. They looked inside the pot, and their eyes lit up.

"Candy!" they cheered.

"Halloween isn't to be feared. . . . It's the greatest night of the year!" Mavis said.

As they dug into their treats, Mavis realized what it all meant. "Wow. So Halloween isn't about death and destruction after all? It's about humans faking being monsters and giving each other candy!"

"But if we're already monsters . . . ," Hank began.

Mavis finished his sentence. ". . . then we can blend right in! We look like human kids in costumes. We can roam around and be free!"

Pedro, Wendy, and Hank found their own makeshift treat bags. Before long they were skipping from house to house, collecting candy from humans who had no idea they were real monsters.

But they didn't notice the creepy jack-o'-lanterns at each house, watching their every move.

CHAPTER THREE

Back at the Vampire Council, there were bright orange pumpkin-shaped lights flashing on a control panel.

"It can only mean one thing," a concerned Council bat told Drac.

"Two-for-one rotten fish tacos in the cafeteria?" Drac asked hopefully.

"That's the green light," the bat said. "Orange is ..."

Drac suddenly remembered. "Monster kids are out trick-or-treating! And then you-know-who will appear!" He shuddered.

Worse, the alert light was close to Hotel Transylvania. He turned into a bat and flew away, determined to catch the little monsters, and fast!

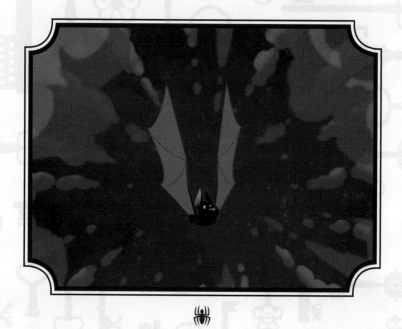

Meanwhile, Mavis and her friends were sitting on a grassy lawn, eating delicious candy.

"I cannot believe we've been lied to all these years!" Mavis commented. "Halloween is amazing! Look at us—we're out in the human world with real humans, and we don't have to hide at all!"

"Plus, candy," Hank said, and everyone agreed.

They didn't notice a bat flying in the distance. It landed on a tree and turned back into Drac. He cringed as he looked around the human village, trying to find the real monsters among all the fakes. Drac

did a double take when he spotted Mavis. "No, it can't be!" He couldn't believe that Mavis was out on the most dangerous night of the year!

27

The four friends had no idea Drac was nearby. Wendy wondered if they should head back to the hotel, but Mavis assured her that they wouldn't get caught. They looked just like everyone else tonight.

Hank pointed at a vampire coming toward them. "Ha! Look at that guy. He looks just like Uncle Drac!" They soon realized that it *was* Drac.

"Mavis . . . ," Drac hissed. He sounded angry but then he hugged Mavis tightly. He was relieved that she was safe, yet he was also furious. "There is literally only one rule on Halloween: Do not go out!"

"Then how come you're out?" Mavis asked.

Drac fumed. "I'm only out to save the disobedient trick-or-treating monsters—who I now know is you. What if you were caught?"

"Dad, how are we gonna get caught when every monster is forcing their kids on lockdown and into hiding?" Mavis asked.

"Not *every* monster," Drac said. He thought of his sister, Lydia. Drac guessed she'd be arriving soon to catch Mavis.

He quickly sent Hank home with his parents, who he had called to pick him up. When Drac spotted Uncle Gene's car in the distance, he tossed Wendy and Pedro toward it so they could go home

too. He needed more time to handle Mavis and the situation. Then he and Mavis turned into bats and flew away.

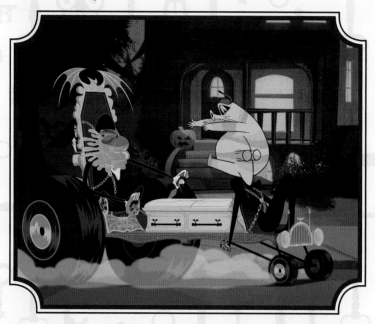

When Drac and Mavis were safely out of sight, they turned back into vampires.

"Whew, that was close. But we must still hide. Danger lurks," Drac insisted.

Mavis wasn't convinced. "Dad, please! What

is so scary about Halloween? Because so far it's been amazing!"

Drac stared off into the distance. "Pumpkin Guts," he admitted.

"Pumpkin Guts?" Mavis asked, but Drac shushed her.

"Shh," he whispered. "I'm about to get all nostalgic and flashback-y." He said that Pumpkin Guts was an

ancient beast who went after monsters who dared to participate in the human ritual of trick-or-treating. He said that for many years, no one knew whether or not the legend was true, but then one little monster got curious and disobeyed the rules. Pumpkin Guts came to the village! Drac shivered. "And now he's risen again, thanks to my own daughter!"

"What does he look like?" Mavis wanted to know.

Drac seemed nervous to even say the word, but he managed. "Pumpkins! All the pumpkins come to life!"

"Pumpkins come to life?" Mavis asked.

Just then, as she said this, the jack-o'-lanterns at every house on the street joined together to form a giant pumpkin-y monster with crackling flames shooting out of its head and arms!

It was Pumpkin Guts! He let out a spine-tingling roar and threw flames at Mavis and Drac, narrowly missing them.

They turned back into bats. Then Pumpkin Guts swatted at them in the air with his pumpkin hands and arms!

Mavis realized she had made a big mistake. Pumpkin Guts *was* real!

CHAPTER FOUR

Mavis and Drac quickly escaped to a nearby forest and turned back into vampires.

"I'm sorry, Dad," Mavis said when they were safe. "I never should have snuck out. I'd better get back home. And you should get back to the Council before they know you're gone."

Drac wished he could, but he said he had to get rid of Pumpkin Guts. "After all, this is kinda, sorta, maybe my fault," he confessed. "I might've left out one tiny detail in the story." Back when Pumpkin

Guts first came to life, *Drac* was the young monster who had gone trick-or-treating on Halloween!

Mavis was shocked that her dad had disobeyed the rules. Still, she couldn't judge him too harshly. She had done the exact same thing. Instead, she asked, "What does Pumpkin Guts want?"

Drac said Pumpkin Guts wanted to turn all monsters into jack-o'-lanterns!

"Each jack-o'-lantern on Halloween was one of his victims. The humans thought it looked all spooky and

kinda ran with it," Drac explained. "I must face him now."

"Not alone you won't," Mavis told him.

Drac was proud of how grown-up his little vampire was and decided to let her help. "We must stop him before he gets there." He pointed toward Hotel Transylvania.

"Holy rabies! The hotel! They'll all be turned into jack-o'-lanterns!" Mavis cried. Then she had an idea. "Wait, does this mean I get to put on a Battle Cloak?"

Drac nodded.

"Boom drac-a-lacka!" Mavis cheered. As she spun around, a red cloak appeared on her shoulders. "Let's fly!"

They turned back into bats and flew toward the hotel.

A short time later, Pumpkin Guts was closer to the hotel, so they tried to distract him.

"Hey," Drac taunted, "over here!"

Pumpkin Guts roared and headed toward them.

"Yikes!" Mavis yelled.

Pumpkin Guts began swatting at them and breathing fire! Then he reached inside his own belly and began throwing slimy, pumpkin-y guts at them.

Mavis was hit and landed on the ground. Drac landed beside her. Then they transformed into vampires once again.

Luckily, Mavis was okay.

"What now?" Drac wondered.

Mavis had an idea. She reached into her pocket and found a piece of Halloween candy. She threw it at Pumpkin Guts. He liked it!

"Look! He wants the candy! Okay, Mavy, give it all you got!" Drac ordered.

Mavis regretted eating all her candy . . . but she knew where she could get some more!

CHAPTER FIVE

Mavis and Drac stood on the bridge that led from the hotel to the human village and yelled at Pumpkin Guts. They wanted him to follow them.

From Uncle Gene's car, Lydia spotted the vampires, too. "Imagine catching both my brother *and* Mavis out on a mandatory lockdown. It's too *bad* to be true!"

Wendy and Pedro were still in the back of the car.

"We've got to help Mavis!" Wendy told Pedro, and they came up with a plan.

Pedro held Wendy over his head. Then Wendy flattened herself out and filled her body with air. She floated like a hot-air balloon, carrying the car and everyone in it with her . . . away from Mavis and Drac!

Meanwhile, Mavis brought Drac to the first house where she trick-or-treated. Drac hugged Mavis as Pumpkin Guts headed toward them.

"I'm sorry, Mavis. I never meant for you to be turned into a pumpkin," he told her. "I failed! Fire, potions, cooties! Monsters have tried everything for thousands of years."

Mavis was calm. "The problem is you've been using the *wrong* kind of monster."

Drac was confused.

The woman opened the front door. "Trick-or-treating is over, hon," she told Mavis, still thinking Mavis was a human in a vampire costume instead of a real vampire. "You and your dad better skedaddle."

Just then, Pumpkin Guts let out a huge roar, and

the woman looked up, noticing Pumpkin Guts for the first time. She quickly grabbed her pumpkin-carving tools and ran out, yelling, "Kitty's got some carving to do!"

She destroyed Pumpkin Guts once and for all . . . while Mavis and Drac escaped!

When it was all over, Mavis didn't want her dad to go back to the Vampire Council. "Are you sure you have to go? That was actually kinda fun," Mavis said, then paused when her dad gave her a stern look. "You know, not the rule-breaking-near-death-thanks-to-a-mythical-creature-I-conjured part, but the working together part," she said sincerely.

Drac thought for a moment. "It *was* kinda fun. But I must go. I have much to do at the

Council," he said, and wrapped his arms around Mavis one more time. "I love you, Mavy. I always will. Now remember, and this is important . . . get back to your room before Lydia finds you!"

Mavis ran toward the hotel while Drac flew back to work.

Aunt Lydia spotted Mavis below the floating car. She turned into a bat and flew after Mavis at top speed.

Mavis reached the lobby first and ran through the crowd of monsters still hunkering down for Halloween. "Excuse me! Coming through!" she said politely.

Moments later Aunt Lydia entered the lobby. She turned back into her vampire form. "Move or die!"

Aunt Lydia commanded, and the monsters cleared a wide aisle to let her float by.

When she reached Mavis's bedroom, Aunt Lydia threw open the door.

Mavis was coming out of the bathroom, wrapped in a bath towel.

"Oh, Aunt Lydia. I didn't hear you come in," Mavis fibbed. "Sorry, I've been in the shower."

Aunt Lydia looked shocked and confused and skeptical all at once. "For ten hours?"

"Has it been that long? Huh," Mavis replied.

"So you've been here all this time?" Aunt Lydia asked, rubbing her eyes.

"Uh-huh," Mavis said casually. "Is the terrible night we must never speak of ever over yet?"

Aunt Lydia nodded. "I think perhaps I should lie down," she said. Her voice was a little shaky. She

hunched over. She was exhausted from the day's events. She floated out of the room.

Mavis spun around and magically changed back into her regular clothes.

"Well, I may have almost been killed by a centuries-old beast that I was kinda responsible for," Mavis said as she looked out the hotel window, "but I also learned the true meaning of Halloween." She smiled. "Candy!"

THE
END